100 No1 Hits

Exclusive Distributors:
Music Sales Limited
8/9 Frith Street,
London W1V 5TZ, England.
Music Sales Pty Limited
120 Rothschild Avenue,
Rosebery, NSW 2018,
Australia.

This book © Copyright 1993
by Wise Publications
Order No.AM90129
ISBN 0-7119-3191-7

Book design by Studio Twenty, London
Compiled by Peter Evans
Music arranged by Peter Lavender
Music processed by MSS Studios

Music Sales' complete catalogue lists thousands of titles and is
free from your local music shop, or direct from Music Sales Limited.
Please send a cheque/postal order for £1.50 for postage to:
Music Sales Limited, Newmarket Road, Bury St. Edmunds, Suffolk IP33 3YB.

Your Guarantee of Quality
As publishers, we strive to produce every book to the
highest commercial standards.
The music has been freshly engraved and the book has
been carefully designed to minimise awkward page turns
and to make playing from it a real pleasure.
Particular care has been given to specifying acid-free,
neutral-sized paper which has not been elemental chlorine bleached
but produced with special regard for the environment.
Throughout, the printing and binding have been planned to
ensure a sturdy, attractive publication which should give
years of enjoyment.
If your copy fails to meet our high standards, please
inform us and we will gladly replace it.

Printed in the United Kingdom by
Redwood Books, Trowbridge, Wiltshire.

Wise Publications
London/New York/Paris/Sydney/Copenhagen/Madrid

A Good Heart *Feargal Sharkey* 122
16 November 1985 (2 weeks)

A Hard Day's Night *The Beatles* 20
23 July 1964 (3 weeks)

A Whiter Shade Of Pale *Procol Harum* 36
8 June 1967 (3 weeks)

A Woman In Love *Barbra Streisand* 98
25 October 1980 (3 weeks)

All I Have To Do Is Dream *Everly Brothers* 9
4 July 1958 (7 weeks)

All You Need Is Love *The Beatles* 38
19 July 1967 (3 weeks)

Always On My Mind *Pet Shop Boys* 132
19 December 1987 (4 weeks)

Amazing Grace *The Royal Scots Dragoon Guards* 53
15 April 1972 (5 weeks)

Annie's Song *John Denver* 59
12 October 1974 (1 week)

Anyone Who Had A Heart *Cilla Black* 14
27 February 1964 (3 weeks)

Bridge Over Troubled Water *Simon & Garfunkel* 48
28 March 1970 (3 weeks)

Bright Eyes *Art Garfunkel* 86
14 April 1979 (6 weeks)

Can't Buy Me Love *The Beatles* 16
2 April 1964 (3 weeks)

Clair *Gilbert O'Sullivan* 54
11 November 1972 (2 weeks)

Claudette *Everly Brothers* 8
4 July 1958 (7 weeks)

Dancing Queen *Abba* 72
4 September 1976 (6 weeks)

Don't Cry For Me Argentina *Julie Covington* 76
17 February 1977 (1 week)

Don't Stand So Close To Me *Police* 96
27 September 1980 (4 weeks)

Ebony And Ivory *Paul McCartney & Stevie Wonder* 106
24 April 1982 (3 weeks)

Eternal Flame *The Bangles* 140
15 April 1989 (4 weeks)

Every Breath You Take *Police* 110
4 June 1983 (4 weeks)

(Everything I Do) I Do It For You *Bryan Adams* 146
13 July 1991 (16 weeks)

Fernando *Abba* 70
8 May 1976 (4 weeks)

Get Off Of My Cloud *The Rolling Stones* 27
4 November 1965 (3 weeks)

Glad All Over *Dave Clark Five* 13
16 January 1964 (2 weeks)

Gonna Make You A Star *David Essex* 62
14 November 1974 (3 weeks)

Good Vibrations *Beach Boys* 32
17 November 1966 (2 weeks)

Goodnight Girl *Wet Wet Wet* 149
19 January 1992 (4 weeks)

Green, Green Grass Of Home *Tom Jones* 33
1 December 1966 (7 weeks)

Hangin' Tough *New Kids On The Block* 142
13 January 1990 (2 weeks)

He Ain't Heavy He's My Brother *The Hollies* 134
24 September 1988 (2 weeks)

Hello Goodbye *The Beatles* 40
6 December 1967 (6 weeks)

Help! *The Beatles* 26
5 August 1965 (3 weeks)

Hey Jude *The Beatles* 44
11 September 1968 (2 weeks)

I Can't Stop Loving You *Ray Charles* 11
12 July 1962 (2 weeks)

I Feel Fine *The Beatles* 17
10 December 1964 (5 weeks)

I Know Him So Well *Barbara Dickson & Elaine Paige* 114
9 February 1985 (4 weeks)

I Think We're Alone Now *Tiffany* 133
30 January 1988 (3 weeks)

I Wanna Dance With Somebody (Who Loves Me) *Whitney Houston* 128
6 June 1987 (2 weeks)

I Want To Wake Up With You *Boris Gardiner* 123
23 August 1986 (3 weeks)

I Will Survive *Gloria Gaynor* 84
17 March 1979 (4 weeks)

I'd Like To Teach The World To Sing *The New Seekers* 52
8 January 1972 (4 weeks)

I'm Not In Love *10CC* 66
28 June 1975 (2 weeks)

I've Got To Get A Message To You *Bee Gees* 43
4 September 1968 (1 week)

If You Leave Me Now *Chicago* 74
16 October 1976 (3 weeks)

Imagine *John Lennon* 103
10 January 1981 (4 weeks)

It's Over *Roy Orbison* 18
25 June 1964 (2 weeks)

Itsy Bitsy, Teenie Weenie, Yellow Polkadot Bikini *Bombalurina* 143
25 August 1990 (3 weeks)

Jealous Guy *Roxy Music* 104
14 March 1981 (2 weeks)

Jumpin' Jack Flash *The Rolling Stones* 42
19 June 1968 (2 weeks)

(Just Like) Starting Over *John Lennon* 100
20 December 1980 (1 week)

Keep On Running *Spencer Davis Group* 28
20 January 1966 (1 week)

Knowing Me, Knowing You *Abba* 78
2 April 1977 (5 weeks)

The Lady In Red *Chris De Burgh* 126
2 August 1986 (3 weeks)

Lady Madonna *The Beatles* 41
27 March 1968 (2 weeks)

Mamma Mia *Abba* 68
31 January 1976 (2 weeks)

Massachusetts *Bee Gees* 37
10 October 1967 (4 weeks)

Memories Are Made Of This *Dean Martin* 6
17 February 1956 (4 weeks)

Merry Xmas Everybody *Slade* 60
15 December 1973 (5 weeks)

Message In A Bottle *Police* 90
29 September 1979 (3 weeks)

Mistletoe And Wine *Cliff Richard* 135
10 December 1988 (4 weeks)

Mr Tambourine Man *Byrds* 25
25 July 1965 (2 weeks)

Mull Of Kintyre *Wings* 80
3 December 1977 (9 weeks)

Ob-La-Di, Ob-La-Da *Marmalade* 46
1 January 1969 (1 week) & 15 January 1969 (2 weeks)

Oh, Pretty Woman *Roy Orbison* 22
8 October 1964 (2 weeks) & 12 November 1964 (1 week)

One Moment In Time *Whitney Houston* 136
15 October 1988 (2 weeks)

Only The Lonely *Roy Orbison* 10
20 October 1960 (2 weeks)

Paint It Black *The Rolling Stones* 29
26 May 1966 (1 week)

Paperback Writer *The Beatles* 31
23 June 1966 (2 weeks)

Pipes Of Peace *Paul McCartney* 112
14 January 1984 (2 weeks)

The Power Of Love *Jennifer Rush* 118
12 October 1985 (5 weeks)

Release Me *Engelbert Humperdinck* 34
2 March 1967 (6 weeks)

Rock Around The Clock *Bill Haley & His Comets* 4
25 November 1955 (3 weeks) & 6 January 1956 (2 weeks)

Sailing *Rod Stewart* 65
6 September 1975 (4 weeks)

Save Your Love *Renée & Renato* 108
18 December 1982 (4 weeks)

Saviour's Day *Cliff Richard* 144
29 December 1990 (1 week)

Sixteen Tons *Tennessee Ernie Ford* 5
20 January 1956 (4 weeks)

Somethin' Stupid *Frank & Nancy Sinatra* 35
13 April 1967 (2 weeks)

Something's Gotten Hold Of My Heart *Marc Almond & Gene Pitney* 138
28 January 1989 (4 weeks)

Spirit In The Sky *Norman Greenbaum* 50
2 May 1970 (2 weeks)

Strangers In The Night *Frank Sinatra* 30
2 June 1966 (3 weeks)

Telstar *Tornados* 12
4 October 1962 (5 weeks)

That'll Be The Day *Crickets* 7
1 November 1957 (3 weeks)

There Must Be An Angel (Playing With My Heart) *Eurythmics* 116
27 July 1985 (1 week)

(This Could Be) The Last Time *The Rolling Stones* 24
18 March 1965 (3 weeks)

This Ole House *Shakin' Stevens* 105
28 March 1981 (3 weeks)

Those Were The Days *Mary Hopkin* 45
25 September 1968 (6 weeks)

Tie A Yellow Ribbon 'Round The Ole Oak Tree *Dawn* 56
21 April 1973 (4 weeks)

Tragedy *Bee Gees* 82
3 March 1979 (2 weeks)

Unchained Melody *Righteous Brothers* 148
3 November 1990 (4 weeks)

Uptown Girl *Billy Joel* 120
5 November 1983 (5 weeks)

Walking On The Moon *Police* 102
8 December 1979 (1 week)

We Don't Talk Anymore *Cliff Richard* 88
25 August 1979 (4 weeks)

Welcome Home (Vivre) *Peters & Lee* 58
21 July 1973 (1 week)

What's Another Year? *Johnny Logan* 92
17 May 1980 (2 weeks)

When The Going Gets Tough, The Tough Get Going *Billy Ocean* 124
8 February 1986 (4 weeks)

Whispering Grass *Windsor Davies & Don Estelle* 64
7 June 1975 (3 weeks)

The Winner Takes It All *Abba* 94
9 August 1980 (2 weeks)

YMCA *Village People* 79
6 January 1979 (3 weeks)

You Win Again *Bee Gees* 130
17 October 1987 (4 weeks)

Rock Around The Clock

Words & Music by Max C. Freedman & Jimmy de Knight

Sixteen Tons

Words & Music by Merle Travis

Memories Are Made Of This

Words & Music by Terry Gilkyson, Richard Dehr & Frank Miller

That'll Be The Day

Words & Music by Norman Petty, Buddy Holly & Jerry Allison

Claudette

Words & Music by Roy Orbison

All I Have To Do Is Dream

Words & Music by Boudleaux Bryant

Only The Lonely

Words & Music by Roy Orbison & Joe Melson

I Can't Stop Loving You

Words & Music by Don Gibson

Telstar

Composed by Joe Meek

Glad All Over

Words & Music by Dave Clark & Mike Smith

Anyone Who Had A Heart

Words by Hal David. Music by Burt Bacharach

Can't Buy Me Love

Words & Music by John Lennon & Paul McCartney

I Feel Fine

Words & Music by John Lennon & Paul McCartney

It's Over

Words & Music by Roy Orbison & Bill Dees

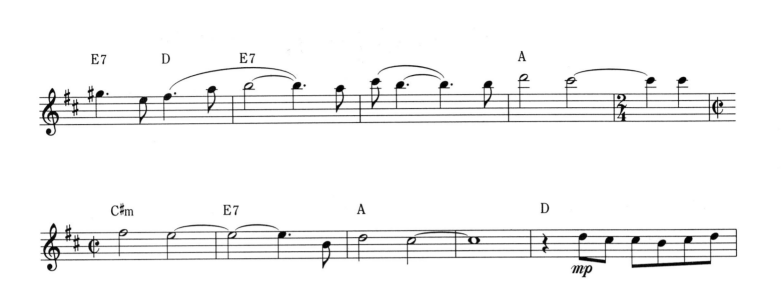

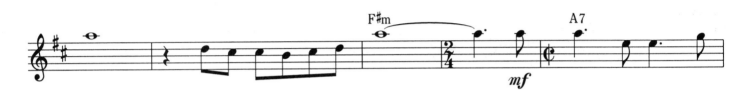

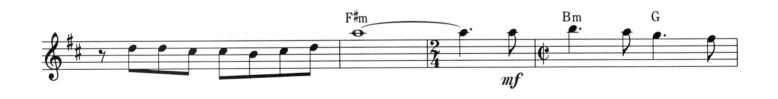

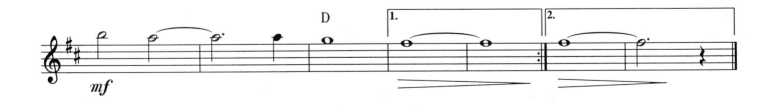

A Hard Days Night

Words & Music by John Lennon & Paul McCartney

Oh, Pretty Woman

Words & Music by Roy Orbison & Bill Dees

This Could Be The Last Time

Words & Music by Mick Jagger & Keith Richards

Mr. Tambourine Man

Words & Music by Bob Dylan

Help!

Words & Music by John Lennon & Paul McCartney

Get Off Of My Cloud

Words & Music by Mick Jagger & Keith Richards

Keep On Running

Words & Music by Jackie Edwards

Paint It Black

Words & Music by Mick Jagger & Keith Richards

Strangers In The Night

Words by Charles Singleton & Eddie Snyder. Music by Bert Kaempfert

Paperback Writer

Words & Music by John Lennon & Paul McCartney

Good Vibrations

Words & Music by Brian Wilson & Mike Love

Green, Green Grass Of Home

Words & Music by Curly Putman

Release Me

Words & Music by Eddie Miller, Dub Williams, Robert Yount & Robert Harris

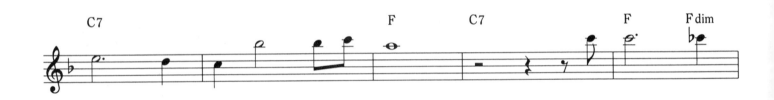

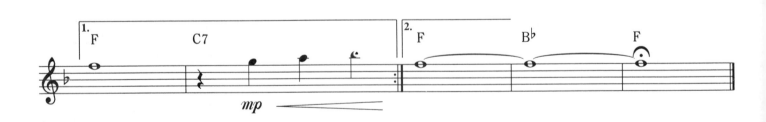

Somethin' Stupid

Words & Music by C. Carson Parks

A Whiter Shade Of Pale

Words & Music by Keith Reid & Gary Brooker

Massachusetts

Words & Music by Barry Gibb, Robin Gibb & Maurice Gibb

All You Need Is Love

Words & Music by John Lennon & Paul McCartney

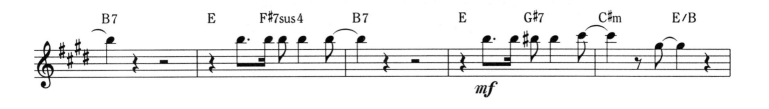

To Coda ⊕

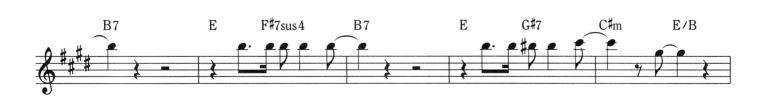

D.S. al Coda　　　　　　　　⊕ **Coda**

Repeat and Fade

Hello Goodbye

Words & Music by John Lennon & Paul McCartney

Lady Madonna

Words & Music by John Lennon & Paul McCartney

Jumpin' Jack Flash

Words & Music by Mick Jagger & Keith Richards

I've Got To Get
A Message To You

Words & Music by Barry Gibb, Robin Gibb & Maurice Gibb

Hey Jude

Words & Music by John Lennon & Paul McCartney

Those Were The Days

Words & Music by Gene Raskin

Ob-La-Di, Ob-La-Da

Words & Music by John Lennon & Paul McCartney

Bridge Over Troubled Water

Words & Music by Paul Simon

Spirit In The Sky

Words & Music by Norman Greenbaum

I'd Like To Teach The World To Sing

Words & Music by Roger Cook, Roger Greenaway, Billy Backer & Billy Davis

Amazing Grace

Traditional adapted by Judy Collins

Clair

Words & Music by Raymond O'Sullivan

Tie A Yellow Ribbon 'Round The Ole Oak Tree

Words & Music by Irwin Levine & L. Russell Brown

Welcome Home

Music by S. Beldone. French Words by Jean Dupré.
English lyrics by Bryan Blackburn

Annie's Song

Words & Music by John Denver

Merry Christmas Everybody

Words & Music by Neville Holder & James Lea

Coda

Gonna Make You A Star

Words & Music by David Essex

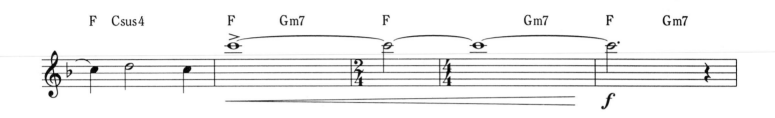

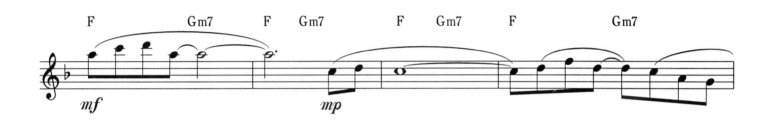

Coda

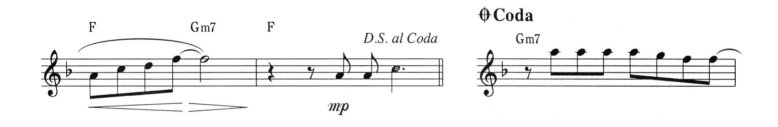

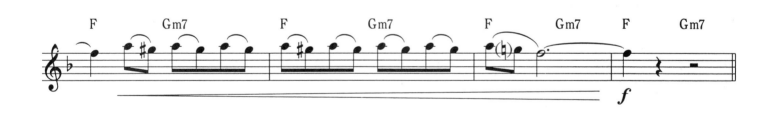

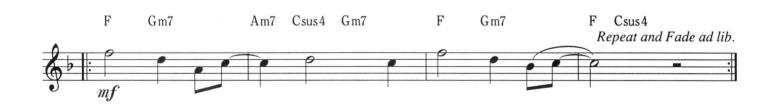

Whispering Grass

Words by Fred Fisher. Music by Doris Fisher

Sailing

Words & Music by Gavin Sutherland

I'm Not In Love

Words & Music by Eric Stewart & Graham Gouldman

Mamma Mia

Words & Music by Benny Andersson, Stig Anderson & Bjorn Ulvaeus

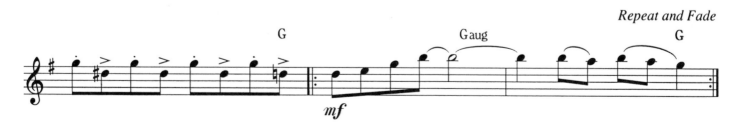

Fernando

Words & Music by Benny Andersson, Stig Anderson & Bjorn Ulvaeus

Dancing Queen

Words & Music by Benny Andersson, Stig Anderson & Bjorn Ulvaeus

If You Leave Me Now

Words & Music by Peter Cetera

75

Don't Cry For Me Argentina

Music by Andrew Lloyd Webber. Lyrics by Tim Rice

poco rall   **Slow tango feel**

To Coda ⊕

⊕ **Coda**

Rall.

D.S. al Coda

Knowing Me, Knowing You

Words & Music by Benny Andersson, Stig Anderson & Bjorn Ulvaeus

YMCA

Words & Music by J. Morali, H. Belolo & V. Willis

Mull Of Kintyre

Words & Music by McCartney & Laine

Tragedy

Words & Music by Barry Gibb, Robin Gibb & Maurice Gibb

I Will Survive

Words & Music by Dino Fekaris & Freddie Perren

Bright Eyes

Words & Music by Mike Batt

Fairly slowly with expression

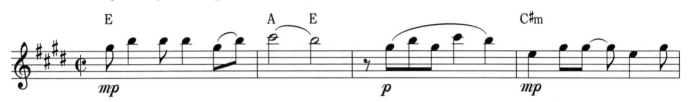

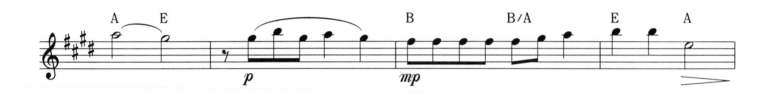

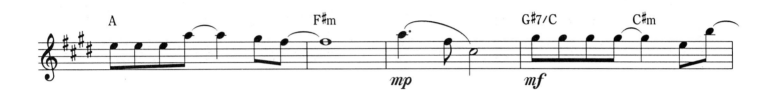

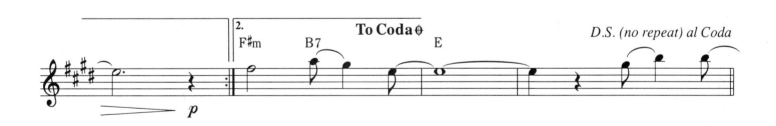

Coda

We Don't Talk Anymore

Words & Music by Alan Tarney

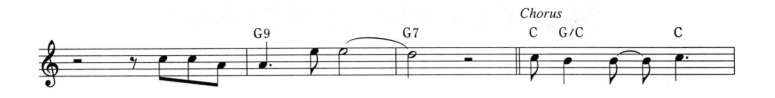

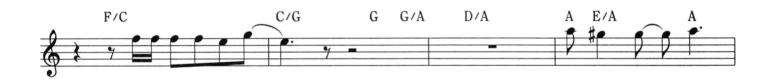

Message In A Bottle

Words & Music by Sting

To Coda ⊕

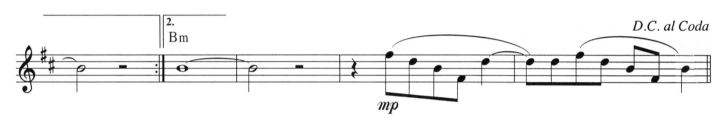

⊕ **Coda**

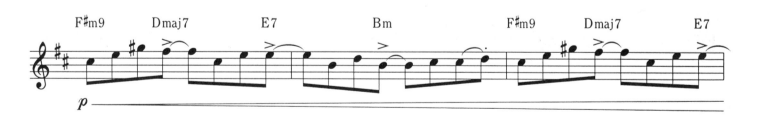

What's Another Year

Words & Music by Shay Healy

The Winner Takes It All

Words & Music by Benny Andersson & Bjorn Ulvaeus

95

Don't Stand So Close To Me

Words & Music by Sting

To Coda ⊕

D.S. al Coda

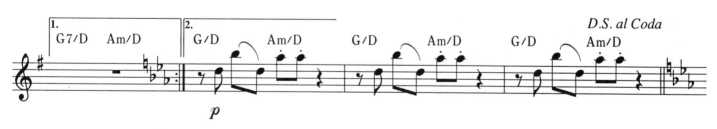

⊕ **Coda**

Repeat to Fade

A Woman In Love

Words & Music by Barry Gibb & Robin Gibb

✪ Coda

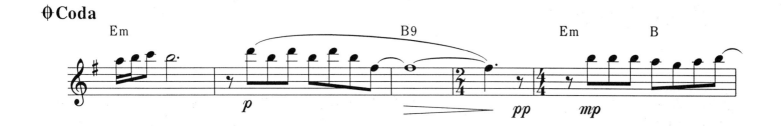

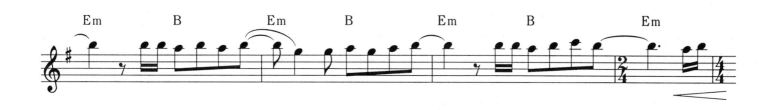

(Just Like) Starting Over

Words & Music by John Lennon

Walking On The Moon

Words & Music by Sting

Imagine

Words & Music by John Lennon

Jealous Guy

Words & Music by John Lennon

This Ole House

Words & Music by Stuart Hamblen

Ebony And Ivory

Words & Music by McCartney

Save Your Love

Words & Music by John & Sue Edward

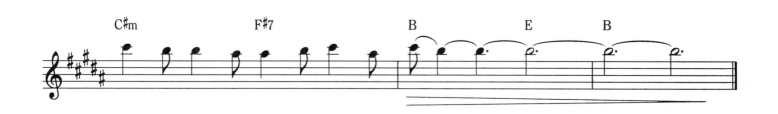

Every Breath You Take

Words & Music by Sting

Pipes Of Peace

Words & Music by McCartney

I Know Him So Well

Words & Music by Benny Andersson, Tim Rice & Bjorn Ulvaeus

There Must Be An Angel
(Playing With My Heart)

Words & Music by A. Lennox & D. A. Stewart

The Power Of Love

Words & Music by C. de Rouge, G. Mende, J. Rush & S. Applegate

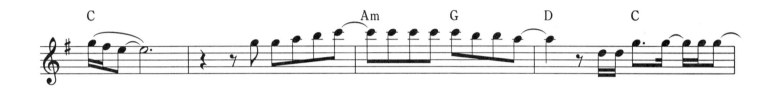

119

Uptown Girl

Words & Music by Billy Joel

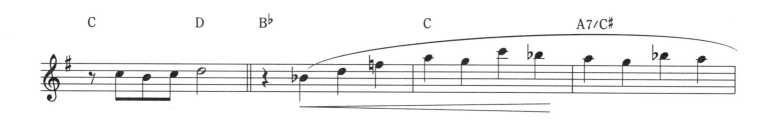
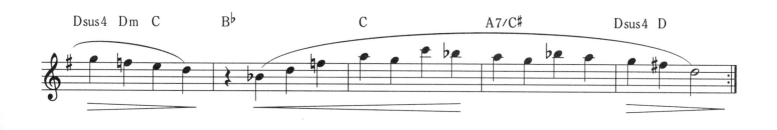
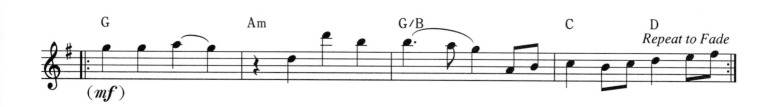

A Good Heart

Words & Music by Maria McKee

I Want To Wake Up With You

Words & Music by Ben Peters

When The Going Gets Tough, The Tough Get Going

Words & Music by Wayne Brathwaite, Barry Eastmond, R.J. Lange & Billy Ocean

The Lady In Red

Words & Music by Chris De Burgh

I Wanna Dance With Somebody
(Who Loves Me)

Words & Music by George Merrill & Shannon Rubicam

You Win Again

Words & Music by Barry Gibb, Robin Gibb & Maurice Gibb

Always On My Mind

Words & Music by Wayne Thompson, Mark James & Johnny Christopher

I Think We're Alone Now

Words & Music by Ritchie Cordell

He Ain't Heavy He's My Brother

Mistletoe And Wine

Music by Keith Strachan. Words by Leslie Stewart & Jeremy Paul

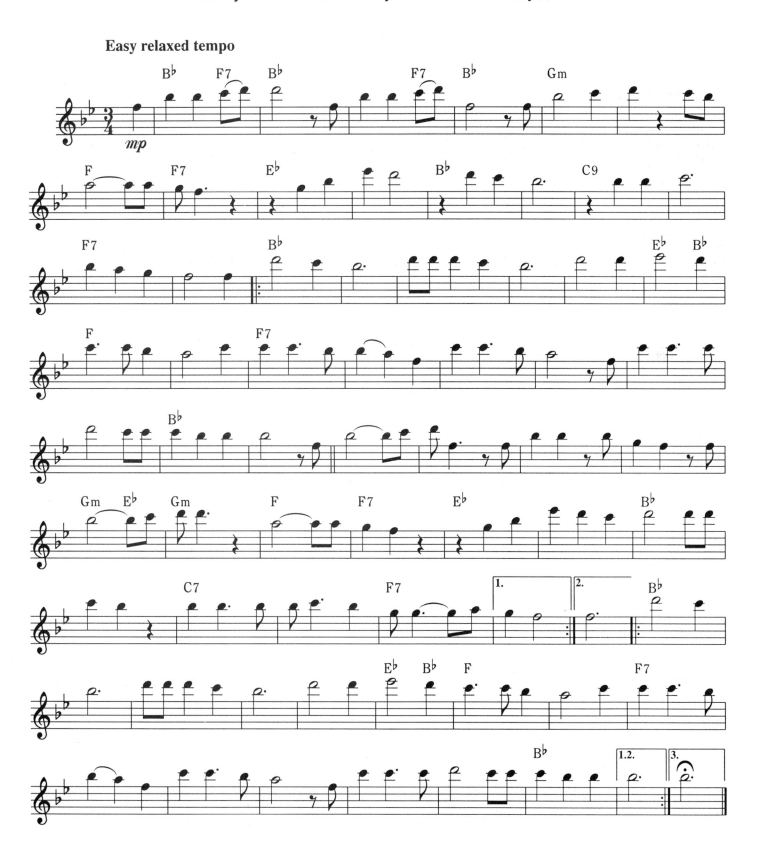

One Moment In Time

Words & Music by Albert Hammond & John Bettis

Something's Gotten
Hold Of My Heart

Words & Music by Roger Cook & Roger Greenaway

Eternal Flame

Words & Music by Billy Steinberg, Tom Kelly & Susanna Hoffs

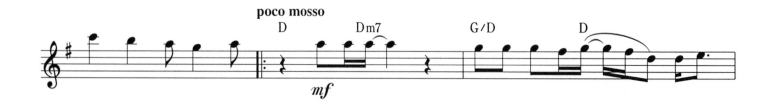

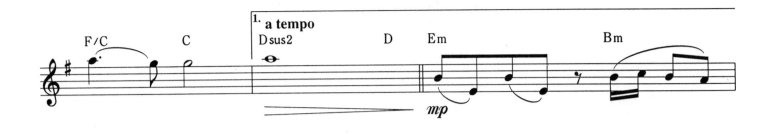

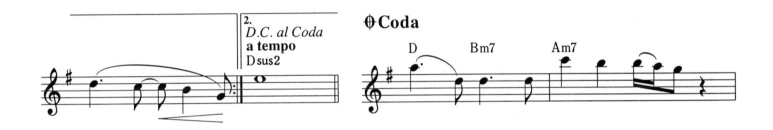

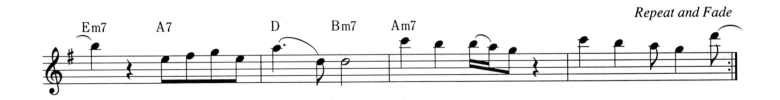

Hangin' Tough

Words & Music by Maurice Starr

Itsy Bitsy, Teenie Weenie Yellow Polkadot Bikini

Words & Music by Lee Pockriss & Paul J. Vance

vocal cue: Two, three, four, tell the peo - ple what she wore.

vocal cue: Two, three, four, Stick a - round we'll tell you more.

Saviour's Day

Words & Music by Chris Eaton

145

(Everything I Do) I Do It For You

Words & Music by Bryan Adams, Michael Kamen & Robert John 'Mutt' Lange

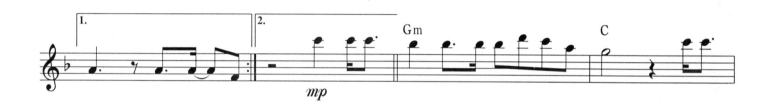

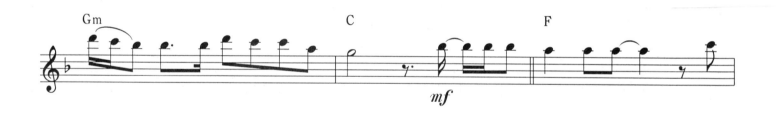

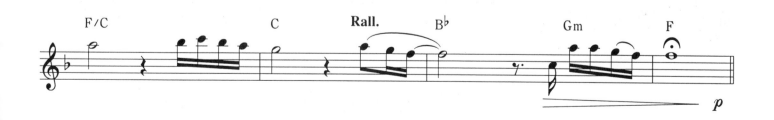

Unchained Melody

Music by Alex North. Words by Hy Zaret.

Goodnight Girl

Words & Music by Clarke, Cunningham, Mitchell & Pellow

1/00(36217)

The Beatles: Music Books In Print

The Best Of The Beatles: Book 1
NO18541

The Best Of The Beatles: Book 2
NO18558

The Best Of The Beatles: Book 3
Sgt. Pepper
NO18566

The Best Of The Beatles : Book 4
NO18608

The Best Of The Beatles: Book 5
NO18616

Beatles Big Note: Piano/Vocal Edition
NO17428

Beatles Big Note: Guitar Edition
NO17402

A Collection Of Beatles Oldies: Piano Vocal Edition
NO17659

A Collection Of Beatles Oldies: Guitar Edition
NO18004

The Beatles Complete: Piano/Vocal/Easy Organ Edition
NO17162

The Beatles Complete (Revised)
Re-engraved, revised edition of 'The Beatles Complete'. For piano/organ/vocal, complete with lyrics and guitar chord symbols. Includes every song composed and recorded by the group. 203 songs, plus 24-page appreciation by Ray Connolly, lavishly illustrated with rare photographs.
Piano/Organ/Vocal Edition
NO18160
Guitar/Vocal Edition
NO18145

The Beatles Bumper Songbook
Full piano/vocal arrangements of 100 songs made famous by the Fab Four. Includes 'All You Need Is Love', 'Yellow Submarine', 'Lucy In The Sky With Diamonds' and 'Hey Jude', all complete with lyrics. 256 pages in all.
NO17998

The Concise Beatles Complete
NO18244

The Beatles Complete: Chord Organ Edition
NO17667

The Beatles Complete: Guitar Edition
NO17303

The Beatles: A Hard Day's Night
NO17576

Beatles For Sale
NO17584

The Beatles: Help
NO17139

The Beatles: Highlights
NO18525

The Beatles: Let It Be
NO17055

The Beatles: Love Songs
NO17915

The Beatles: Magical Mystery Tour
NO17600

The Beatles 1962-1966
NO17931

The Beatles 1967-70
NO17949

The Beatles: Revolver
NO17568

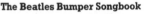

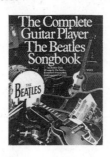

The Beatles

Enya

Phil Collins

Van Morrison

Bob Dylan

Sting

Paul Simon

Tracy Chapman

Eric Clapton

Pink Floyd

New Kids On The Block

Bryan Adams

Tina Turner

Elton John

Bee Gees

Whitney Houston

AC/DC

Bringing you the words

All the latest in rock and pop. Plus the brightest and best in West End show scores. Music books for every instrument under the sun. And exciting new teach-yourself ideas like "Let's Play Keyboard" - in cassette/book packs, or on video. Available from all good music shops.

and music

Music Sales' complete catalogue lists thousands of titles and is available free from your local music shop, or direct from Music Sales Limited. Please send a cheque or postal order for £1.50 (for postage) to:

Music Sales Limited
Newmarket Road,
Bury St Edmunds,
Suffolk IP33 3YB

Buddy

Five Guys Named Moe

Les Misérables

West Side Story

Phantom Of The Opera

Show Boat

The Rocky Horror Show

Bringing you the world's best music.